Waltham Forest Libraries

Please return this item by the last date stamped. The loan may be renewed unless required by another customer.

ILLUSTRATED BY **SOFIA CARDOSO**

D0270655

Meet the Clamerkin Clan

Amy and her friends love solving problems on the Island of Clamerkin, helped by Amy's secret ability to talk to animals!

Amy

Amy's magic necklace

Plato

Hilton

Einstein

Isambard

Willow

Bun

First published in the UK in 2019 by Usborne Publishing Ltd., Usborne House, 83-85 Saffron Hill, London EC1N 8RT, England. www.usborne.com

Text copyright © Diana Kimpton, 2019

The right of Diana Kimpton to be identified as the author of this work has been asserted by her in accordance with the Copyright, Designs and Patents Act, 1988.

Illustration copyright © Usborne Publishing Ltd., 2019

Illustrations by Sofia Cardoso.

Illustration p110-111 taken from *Look and Find Cats and Dogs* by Kirsteen Robson and Gareth Lucas © Usborne Publishing Ltd., 2016

The name Usborne and the devices ♀♁ are Trade Marks of Usborne Publishing Ltd.

A CIP catalogue record for this book is available from the British Library.

JFMAM JASOND/19 05258/1 ISBN 9781474960267 Printed in the UK.

CHAPTER 1

"Look, Hilton," said Amy Wild, pointing at a row of small houses. "Mrs Taylor lives in the one with the white fence." She didn't bother to mention the seagulls sitting on the roof. Even here in the middle of town, there were always gulls around, because everywhere on Clamerkin Island was close to the sea.

The cairn terrier trotting beside her gave a small whimper. "Do we have to go there?" he grumbled. "I want to go to Home Meadow and chase sticks."

Amy wasn't surprised to hear the dog talking. The magic necklace she was wearing gave her the power to understand what animals were saying. "We'll play afterwards," she promised.

"After what?" barked Hilton.

"After I've delivered this book that Granty is lending Mrs Taylor. It's about puppy training."

Mrs Taylor spotted them coming and met them at the gate. She was tall and slim with short, white hair, metal-rimmed glasses and a worried expression. She looked relieved when

Amy handed her the book. "Thank you. That's perfect," she said, as she flicked through the pages. "Little Martha is my very first puppy so I'm not sure what I should be doing. She's adorable and I love her to bits, but she is very hard work."

As she spoke, a small bundle of white fluff bounded out of the front door and hurtled down the path towards them. "Iggle, oggle, din-dins," yapped the puppy. Amy's secret power wasn't much help with Martha. She was still a baby so she hadn't learned to talk yet.

Amy bent down and held out her hand. Martha rushed up to it, wagging her stubby white tail. But she stopped as soon as she noticed Hilton.

Martha bounced over to him and gazed up into his face. "Iggle, oggle, din-dins," she yapped again. Then she rolled on her back and waved her paws in the air. Her words didn't make sense, but Amy could see that she wanted to play.

Hilton obviously understood too. He gave the puppy a playful shove with his nose to get her back on her feet and wagged his tail in greeting. Unfortunately, Martha misunderstood. Instead of wagging her own tail in response, she tried to catch Hilton's.

The terrier turned in a circle, trying to keep his rear end away from the lively puppy. But Martha seemed to think this was part of the game. She yapped in excitement as she chased his tail and finally succeeded in giving it a playful nip.

Her teeth were very small, but they were also very sharp.

"Ouch!" said Hilton. "Puppy games hurt." He pushed Martha away with his paw and turned to Amy. "I'll meet you down the road when you've finished," he said. Then he trotted out of the gate.

Martha tried to follow, but Amy was too quick for her. She grabbed hold of the puppy and whisked her off the ground.

"Well done!" said Mrs Taylor. Then she looked anxiously after Hilton and added, "Will your dog be all right without you?" She hadn't understood what he'd said – she'd just heard barking.

"He'll be fine," said Amy, as she struggled to keep hold of the squirming ball of white fur. "I'll catch him up in minute." Then Martha stopped wriggling and started sniffing the hands that held her.

Amy braced herself, ready to pull her fingers away if the puppy nipped them. But she didn't. She licked them instead. Her tongue was very small, very pink and very tickly. It made Amy giggle.

Suddenly she heard Hilton barking in the distance. "Come quickly," he called. "There's something wrong with Bun."

Amy didn't hesitate. "I've got to go," she said, as she thrust Martha into Mrs Taylor's arms. Then she raced off to find Hilton, calling goodbye as she went.

He was waiting for her beside a large bush growing close to a garden wall. But there was no sign of Bun – the fat black cat from the baker's shop.

"What's going on?" Amy asked.

"I don't know," said Hilton. "But Bun is really upset. Come and see for yourself." He disappeared under the bush, obviously expecting her to follow.

That wasn't easy, because Amy was much bigger than a cairn terrier. She wished she could just walk around to the other side, but she couldn't because of the wall. So she had to lie on her tummy and wriggle underneath the branches by pushing herself along the ground with her feet. Twigs snagged at her hair and caught on her clothes, but she eventually managed to squeeze in beside Hilton. That's when she spotted Bun lying on the dusty ground.

Amy had never seen him looking so miserable. His ears lay flat and his whiskers drooped.

"What are you doing here?" he asked.

"I think *we* should be asking *you* that," said Amy.

"I'm hiding because I'm unhappy," Bun whimpered. "No one likes me, and I don't have any friends."

"Yes, you do," said Hilton. "I like you and so does Amy."

"And so does everyone else in the Clamerkin Clan," added Amy. She hoped it would cheer Bun up to remind him of the group of animals they were all part of. But it didn't. It made him even more upset.

He opened his mouth wide and wailed in distress. "The other cats in the clan don't like me any more. They say I'm horrid and nasty and a thief. And they told me to go away. So I have."

Amy was astonished. Everyone in the clan had been friends until now. That's how they managed to work together so well to solve problems on the island where they lived. "What's gone wrong?" she asked, as she reached forward and tickled Bun under his chin.

"And why do they say you're a thief?" added Hilton.

Bun gave a deep sigh. "Someone is stealing their dinners, and they all think it's me."

"Why?" asked Amy. The black cat loved food and was always hungry. But she'd never known him to steal from his friends before.

"It's because no one is stealing my food," said Bun. "The others say that proves I'm the thief."

Hilton looked thoughtful. "It does seem a bit suspicious."

"But it's definitely not proof," said Amy. "Come on! We'd better find out what's really going on."

CHAPTER 2

Amy backed carefully out of the bush, and Bun slunk after her with his tail so low that it dragged on the ground. When she was in the open, she stood up, brushed the dirt off her clothes and picked up the cat. He nestled into her arms and mewed softly as he rested his head on her shoulder.

"What are we going to do?" asked Hilton.

"You're going to run on ahead and call an emergency clan meeting. I'll bring Bun – you organize the others."

The terrier raced away and disappeared under a nearby fence. Being a dog gave him the advantage of being able to take shortcuts that Amy couldn't use. He could also run faster than her, even though his legs were so much shorter.

Luckily Amy didn't need to run. Even walking was hard work while she was carrying the cat. Bun wasn't just sad, he was also very heavy. But Amy didn't want to put him down. Being cuddled seemed to make him a little bit happier.

She plodded back past Mrs Taylor's house and the shops in the main street. By the time she reached the Primrose Tea Room where she lived, her arms ached so much that she needed a break. But she'd also thought of another way to cheer Bun up.

"Have we any sardines?" she asked, as she stepped into the kitchen. She nearly collided with her mum, who was just leaving with a tray of cakes.

"Don't bring that cat in here," said Mum. "It's unhygienic."

Bun shrank down into the safety of Amy's arms. "She doesn't like me either," he whimpered.

"Something wrong, love?" asked Amy's great-aunt when Mum had gone. "I imagine that's why you've got the baker's cat with you."

Amy nodded. Granty was the person who had given her the magic necklace, and she was the only other human in the world who knew about its secret power. She knew about the clan too, so Amy knew she'd understand. "Bun's feeling sad," she explained. "So I thought his favourite food might cheer him up."

"I don't think it will," moaned the black cat. But he brightened up a little when Granty carried a sardine on a saucer into the garden.

Amy put him on the ground in front of it and waited while he gobbled it up. That didn't take long. Bun ate  faster than any other cat Amy had ever met.

"Come on," she said, as he licked the last traces from his lips. "Time for the meeting."

But Bun didn't move. He crouched close to the ground and stared at her with big, sad eyes. "I don't want to go. They'll be horrid again."

"You've got to come," said Amy. "We can't sort this out unless you do." She set off down the garden, patting her leg to encourage him to follow.

"I suppose I don't have much choice," Bun muttered. He rose unwillingly to his feet and slunk along beside her, keeping as close to her as he could.

At the far end of the garden, Amy and Bun slipped between the bushes until they reached the clearing in the middle that was the clan's almost-secret hideout. The rest of the clan were already there. Hilton ran towards her, wagging his tail. Plato the parrot squawked a welcome from his perch on one of the branches. But the three other cats stared at Bun with narrowed eyes.

Willow, the Siamese from the post office, arched her back and stuck her tail straight up in the air, the hairs sticking out like a bottlebrush. "What have you brought *him* for?" she hissed.

Bun backed away and hid behind Amy's legs. "You see what I mean?" he whispered. "They don't like me at all."

"Don't worry," Amy whispered back. "I'll sort this out." Then she stared firmly at the other three cats and said, "Bun has every right to be here. He's a member of the clan."

"But he shouldn't be after what he's done," said Isambard. He was a tabby cat with rather grubby paws and a passion for machinery.

"Thieves aren't allowed in the clan," added Einstein – the white Persian cat from the school. "And Bun is a thief. He keeps stealing my dinner."

"And mine," said Willow.

"Mine too," said Isambard.

"It's not me!" wailed Bun.

Einstein scowled at him. "It must be you. Why else would our food keep  being stolen but not yours?"

Plato tapped his beak on the tree trunk to

attract attention. "I watch lots of detective programmes on TV, and the thief is never the one most people suspect."

"That's just stories," said Willow. "This is real life."

"But stories can be useful," said Einstein, who loved listening to them at school.

"And Plato's made a good point," said Amy. She waited while the parrot fluffed out his feathers proudly. Then she continued, "Although you *think* it's obvious that Bun is the thief, that doesn't make it true."

"Exactly," said Plato. "We need to investigate."

"How?" asked Hilton.

Amy thought for a moment. "Let's start by looking at when the food is stolen."

"It's always at night," said Isambard. The other two cats nodded in agreement. "In the dark," said Einstein. "When we're asleep or we're out," added Willow. Hilton stared at them in disbelief. "You mean, you leave food in your bowls? You don't eat it all as soon as you're given it?"

Willow stuck her nose in the air. "Of course we don't eat everything at once. We're cats — not dogs. We sniff at our food,

take a few dainty bites, and then go away and come back to it later."

Bun's eyes opened wide in surprise. "I don't do that. I always eat all my food straight away."

"He's right," said Amy. "I just watched him do that with a sardine." Then she thought for a moment and added, "Maybe that's the reason his food isn't stolen."

"I suppose it might be," said Isambard. "But that still doesn't prove he's not the thief."

"He could be stealing our food after he's eaten his own," Willow suggested.

"He *is* always hungry," added Einstein.

"But it's not me!" wailed Bun.

He gazed pleadingly at Amy. "How can I prove I'm innocent?"

Plato tossed his head in exasperation. "You shouldn't have to. According to what I've heard on TV, it's up to them to prove you're guilty."

"Stop interfering, you silly bird," said Willow. "It's nothing to do with you."

Hilton jumped to his feet and gave a low growl. "Don't be rude to Plato. He's only trying to help."

"But it's not him who's going hungry," said Isambard.

Amy wondered if it was hunger that was making the three cats so cross and unreasonable. She'd never seen them like this before, and she didn't like it at all. She needed to do something

quickly to stop her friends
falling out with each other so
badly that they
could never
make up.

Amy took
a deep breath,
stood up straight
and clapped her
hands for attention. The
argument stopped abruptly,
and six pairs of eyes stared
at her. When she was
sure everyone was
listening, she said,
"We need to set
a trap."

CHAPTER 3

The rest of the clan stared intently at Amy as she started to explain her plan. "It's simple," she said. "Tonight I want all four of you cats to leave some food in your bowls for the thief to steal."

Bun's mouth dropped open in astonishment. "Even me?"

"Yes. Even you," Amy said firmly. "That's important. The plan won't work properly unless you do."

Bun stood up straight and stared at Amy with a very determined expression on his face. "I'll do it. I promise."

Isambard narrowed his eyes and licked his paw thoughtfully. "I don't understand. You're only asking us to do what we do every night anyway."

"No, I'm not," said Amy with a smile. "This time you are all going to stay indoors and stay awake and watch what happens."

"That's clever," said Hilton. "They'll see who the thief is."

"And they can tell the rest of us tomorrow," said Plato.

Next morning, Amy got up early and ran down to the almost-secret hideout before she left for school. She was so sure her plan would have worked that she expected the cats to be full of excitement. But they weren't. Bun was half-asleep and busy yawning. The other three were sitting together, with their backs to him. They looked less tired than him, but very cross and very hungry.

She kneeled down on the grass between Bun and the other cats. Hilton and Plato sat close beside her, eager to hear what had happened the night before.

"You first, Bun," she said. "Did you leave some of your food last night?"

"Yes," said the black cat proudly. "I knew how much it mattered."

"Did you stay awake all night?"

"Yes," he said, with such a big yawn that Amy wondered if he would manage to stay awake for the rest of the conversation.

"What about the food?" said Plato. "Was it still there in the morning?"

Bun shook his head and yawned again. "No," he said sleepily. "It had all gone. The bowl was licked completely clean."

"All our food was stolen again too," said Einstein. The three cats crept closer, eager to hear what Bun had discovered.

Amy was excited too. "So who came in?" she asked.

"No one," said Bun in a very subdued voice. He looked at Amy with mournful eyes. "I'm really sorry. I got a bit peckish at midnight and ate it all myself.

Willow huffed with annoyance. "You see. It *is* him. He just can't resist food."

"But it was mine anyway," said Bun. "I wasn't stealing it."

Amy was worried another argument was about to start, so she quickly turned to Willow and asked, "Did you see who took your food last night?"

The Siamese cat looked embarrassed.

"Not exactly," she said.

Hilton gave a snort of disapproval. "Did you go to sleep?"

"Only for a little while," she mewed. "It's so hard to stay awake when your eyes are heavy and droopy. And when I woke up, the food wasn't there any more."

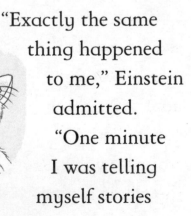

"Exactly the same thing happened to me," Einstein admitted. "One minute I was telling myself stories

to keep me awake. The next thing
I knew it was getting light, and the
food had gone."

"That's not surprising," said Plato.
"I heard on TV that cats sleep fifteen
to twenty hours a day."

"It would help if they didn't," said
Hilton.

Amy looked despairingly at
Isambard. He was her last chance.
"How about you?
Did you go to
sleep as well?"

"Absolutely
not," the tabby
cat replied. "I
stayed awake for
the whole night."

Then he gave an embarrassed cough
and added, "But I didn't stay indoors.
I heard this aeroplane flying overhead,
and I couldn't resist going out to see it.
Wonderful things aeroplanes. Then
I saw a shooting star, and I had to stay
outside in case there was another one."

"So you didn't see
the thief either,"
said Hilton with
a sigh. He
looked at Amy
and asked,
"What are we
going to do now?"
Amy didn't know.
She'd been so sure that her plan would
work that she hadn't thought of any

other ideas. Now she needed to come up with another one fast, before the cats started quarrelling again.

Luckily Plato came to her rescue. "TV detectives always examine the scene of the crime."

"Why?" asked Bun.

"To look for clues. Stray hairs. Footprints. That sort of thing."

Willow stared suspiciously at Bun. "I bet you all the hairs are black," she muttered.

Amy ignored the Siamese cat. "Plato's idea is brilliant," she said. "We'll search the homes of all the cats who have had their food stolen to see what we can find."

"Who's going to do the searching?"

asked Hilton. "We can't all go. We'd attract too much attention from their humans."

There was a long pause while they all thought. The cats licked their paws, Plato and Hilton stared at the sky and Amy chewed the edge of her thumbnail. Then Isambard said, "I think Amy should do it. She's got hands. Wonderful things, hands, especially for searching. And she can talk to humans as well. That's another useful skill."

The cats nodded their agreement. But Plato was disappointed at being left out. "It was my idea in the first place," he argued.

"I'd be useful too," said Hilton.

"I could use my nose to sniff out clues."

"I'll take you both with me if I can," Amy promised. "But I might not be able to do it every time."

Suddenly Willow's eyes opened wide in alarm. "How are you going to get into our homes to do the searching? You can't tell our humans what you're doing without giving away the fact that you can talk to animals."

Amy bit her lip anxiously. She knew the Siamese cat was right. The necklace's magic powers had to stay secret to stop anyone misusing them.

So she needed to think of a way to do her detective work without attracting attention. And she needed to do it quickly, before the disagreement between the cats split the clan apart.

CHAPTER 4

Everyone agreed that it made sense to search Einstein's home first. He lived at the school, and Amy had to go there anyway. In fact, she'd be in trouble if she didn't, so the meeting came to a sudden end to stop her being late.

She ran all the way to school and managed to get there just as the bell rang. There was no sign of Einstein

as she followed the rest of the Juniors into their classroom. He wasn't there during the first two lessons either. But the white cat rubbed himself against her legs as she went out for break. "Come on," he said. "Let's do the search now."

Amy started to follow him down the corridor, but she suddenly realized that she didn't know where she was going. "Whereabouts in the school do you get fed?" she asked.

"In the storeroom," Einstein replied.

Amy gulped. "Students aren't allowed in there without permission. I'll get into trouble if I'm caught."

"And us cats will be in trouble if we don't find the thief. I'm already getting thinner and so are Willow and Isambard."

"Okay," said Amy, as she summoned all her courage. "Lead the way, but let's be careful."

They had nearly reached the storeroom door when a voice behind them asked, "Where are you going?" It was Amy's teacher, Mrs Damson.

Amy hesitated while she tried to think of a good excuse. Then she said, "I was having a walk," in what she hoped was a convincing voice.

It obviously wasn't. Mrs Damson's eyes narrowed with suspicion. "This is a very strange place to be walking," she said. "Now go into the playground with the others and have your exercise there."

Amy turned and walked away with her shoulders slumped in disappointment. She went as slowly as she could in the hopes that she might be able to double back when her teacher lost interest. But she didn't get a chance. Mrs Damson watched her closely all the way along the corridor and made sure she went outside as she'd been told.

The rest of the morning was so busy with lessons that there wasn't another chance to search until lunchtime. Amy waited until the rest of her class were busy eating their sandwiches, then she slipped out of the assembly hall and set off towards the storeroom with Einstein. Surely they wouldn't be caught this time – Mrs Damson would be in the staffroom eating her own lunch.

This time they reached the storeroom door without being caught. Amy reached out for the handle but, before she could touch it, a man's voice rang out. "Amy Wild. What are you doing?" It was Mr Plimstone, the head teacher.

Amy swallowed hard and tried not to panic. "I was just…um…looking for my friend," she said, with her fingers crossed behind her back. She hoped he wouldn't ask which friend it was.

Mr Plimstone raised his eyebrows and peered down his nose at her. "I don't think she's likely to be in there, is she?"

"No," said Amy in a very quiet voice. She shifted awkwardly from foot to foot, wondering what was going to happen next. She'd never been punished by the head teacher before, and she wasn't looking forward to it.

Luckily, at that moment, the school secretary called from the office, "Mr Plimstone! You're wanted on the phone."

The head teacher sighed and waved his hand towards the playground. "Off you go then, Amy. And don't let me catch you here again."

"Phew! That was close," said Einstein as they walked away. "Perhaps we should give up."

"But we can't," said Amy. "We just need to find a way to get permission to go to the storeroom."

She still hadn't thought of one when lessons started again. Mrs Damson was teaching the class about the way times vary around the world, using an enormous globe that revolved on its stand and a torch to represent the sun. When she finished, she said, "I need a volunteer to take the globe back to the storeroom for me."

This chance was too good to miss. Amy's hand shot into the air faster than anyone else's and, to her relief, she was given the job. It was more difficult than she'd expected. The globe was heavier than it looked and very awkward to carry. She had to put it on the floor while she opened the storeroom door.

"We'd better search quickly," she told Einstein, as they stepped inside. "I need to get back before Mrs Damson gets suspicious." She put the globe on the shelf where it belonged. Then she followed the white cat past the piles of equipment to the place where he ate and slept.

Amy looked around carefully. There were two bowls on the floor, one empty and one full to the brim with water. "It looks as if the thief wasn't thirsty," said Amy.

Beside the bowls was a cat basket with a comfy cushion. Between the bowls and the basket was a patch of very dusty floor and, in the dust, was a paw print. Amy could hardly believe how easy it was to be a detective. "Look, Einstein!" she said, pointing proudly at her discovery. "It's a clue."

"No, it's not," said Einstein. "That's mine." He put his front foot carefully on the paw print – it matched exactly.

Amy tried not to feel too disappointed. She stood up and looked around again. "I wonder how the thief gets in."

"Through there," said Einstein, pointing at a cat flap in another door

that led to the outside world. "All the doors to the school are locked at night. My cat flap is the only way in and out."

Amy stared thoughtfully at the flap. "Do you think Bun could get through here? It's not very big and he is rather fat."

"Of course he could," said Einstein. "Cats are very bendy, even fat ones. It might be a bit of a squeeze, but he could definitely get through."

Amy was disappointed. For a moment, she thought she'd discovered a reason why Bun couldn't be the thief. But she hadn't. So she went up the steps and examined the flap carefully. At first, she thought there was nothing there. Then she spotted a single hair caught in the hinge. "Look!" she said. "This really is a clue."

"I don't think so," said Einstein, shaking himself so his fluffy coat stuck out in all directions. "That hair is white and so are all of mine."

"Bother!" said Amy. Being a detective was more difficult than it looked on TV. If her other searches were as unsuccessful as this one, they might never discover who was stealing the food.

CHAPTER 5

Hilton and Plato were waiting for Amy when she got back from school. They followed her up to her bedroom, demanding to know what she'd found in Einstein's home. And they weren't pleased with her reply.

"Nothing at all?" repeated Hilton in disbelief. "Surely a thief can't rob somewhere without leaving any clues."

"They might if they're very clever," said Plato.

"Or very lucky," added Amy. She changed out of her school clothes and took some pocket money from her piggy bank. "Come on," she said. "Perhaps we'll do better in the other searches."

"Which one's next?" asked Plato.

"Willow's home," said Amy.

She didn't go straight to the post office where Willow lived. Instead she walked to the only flower shop in town, with Hilton by her side and Plato perched on her shoulder.

"Why have we come here?" asked the cairn terrier.

"To get an excuse to visit Willow," Amy explained. She went inside, bought a pretty bunch of flowers, and set off to the post office with them.

"I still don't understand," said Plato.

"You will," said Amy. "Just wait and see."

The post office was busy as usual. Amy had to wait in a line of customers

until it was her turn to talk to the postmistress, Miss Pickle.

"I've bought you a present," said Amy, holding up the bunch of flowers. "I thought the ones Granty and I gave you last week might be a bit old by now."

Miss Pickle was delighted. "How very kind," she said with a smile. Then she glanced anxiously around the shop. There was still a long queue of people at the counter, waiting for her to serve them. "But those flowers need to go in water, and I can't do it now. I'm too busy."

That was exactly what Amy had hoped would happen. "I'll do it for you," she said. "And I'll say hello to

Willow at the same time."

Miss Pickle gave a sigh of relief.
"That would be really useful. You can
use the vase that's on the kitchen
window sill." Then she looked at
Hilton and Plato and added, "I'm
afraid you'll have to leave your dog
and parrot outside. My cousin is
coming to stay, and she is very allergic
to dogs and feathers."

"I don't drop feathers," Plato
squawked in protest. "I'm a very tidy
parrot." But only Amy understood
what he was saying. She took him and
Hilton outside and left them there.
Then she went into the private part of
the post office, where Willow and Miss
Pickle lived.

She was disappointed not to have
Hilton with her to sniff out clues. But
as soon as she stepped through the
door, she realized he wouldn't have
found any. The whole place was
spotlessly clean and smelled strongly of
bleach and disinfectant.

"I'm sorry," said Willow as she
jumped down from the sofa where she'd
been dozing. "My human has a visitor
coming so she's gone mad on cleaning.
Even if the thief did leave some clues,
I don't think they'll still be here."

"Don't worry," said Amy, as she
tickled the cat behind her ears. Then
she checked everywhere just to be sure.
Willow had two bowls like Einstein —
one for food and one for water. She also

had a comfy bed with a velvet cushion and a cat flap in the back door that gleamed with polish. But there were no footprints, no stray hairs and no other clues.

Amy found the vase, filled it with water and put the flowers in it as she'd promised. Then she went outside and told Plato and Hilton the bad news.

They were just as disappointed as she was.

"I hope we find something at Isambard's place," said Plato. "It's our last chance."

"Let's go home first," said Amy. "I need to fetch something." She led them back to the Primrose Tea Room and went inside. Then she came out again, holding something in a small bag and a piece of paper.

Hilton sniffed at the bag. "What's in there?" he asked. "It smells nice."

"You'll see," said Amy, as she pushed the piece of paper into her pocket. "Now let's go."

When they reached the workshop where Isambard lived, they found his human lying underneath a car he was mending. Only his feet were sticking out.

Amy bent down beside them and peered into the darkness. "Hello, Mr Jones," she called. "I've brought you something."

Mr Jones slid out from under the car and grinned at her. His teeth looked extra white against the smears of black oil on his face. "Thanks, love," he said, as Amy handed him the bag. Then he peeped inside, and his grin grew wider. "Oooh! Lemon drizzle cake. That's my favourite."

"I'm glad you're pleased," said Amy. "Can I say hello to Isambard while I'm here?"

"Course you can," he said, with his mouth full of cake. He waved his hand towards an open door at the back of the workshop. "He's probably through there."

Amy, Hilton and Plato discovered that the doorway led into a storeroom filled with a jumble of boxes, tins and pieces of car. It was far less tidy than Einstein's home and much dirtier than Willow's. Isambard ran to greet them. "I've been waiting for you. I hope you're going to find some clues."

"So do we," said Amy. "We haven't had much luck anywhere else."

Plato flew over to the outside door. "Look! He's got a cat flap, just like Willow and Einstein. I'll check it for trapped hairs."

"And I'll check the floor for smells," said Hilton. He rushed back and forth with his nose close to the floor and his tail wagging rapidly.

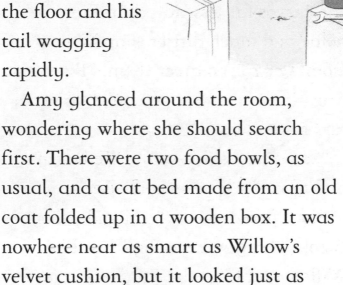

Amy glanced around the room, wondering where she should search first. There were two food bowls, as usual, and a cat bed made from an old coat folded up in a wooden box. It was nowhere near as smart as Willow's velvet cushion, but it looked just as comfortable.

Suddenly Hilton barked, "Dog! I smell dog."

"A clue!" Plato squawked in delight.

Amy was excited too. Were they finally on their way to solving the mystery?

CHAPTER 6

"Where can you smell dog?" Amy asked Hilton.

"Everywhere, I expect," said Isambard in a rather bored voice. "My human's brother comes here every day with his dog. She's got black spots all over her white coat, but they don't seem to be catching."

"That means she knows where your

food is," said Amy, as she gazed thoughtfully at the door. "Maybe she comes back at night and steals it."

Isambard shook his head. "She's much too big to get through the cat flap, and that's the only way in when the workshop is locked."

"But Amy's hit on something important," said Plato. "The thief doesn't have to be a cat. It could be some other animal that is small enough to get through the flap."

"A weasel?" suggested Isambard.

"No," said Hilton. "I can't smell one."

"A rat?" said Plato.

"Nope," said Hilton.

"How about a hedgehog?" suggested

Amy. "I read somewhere that they like cat food."

"I definitely can't smell one of those," said Hilton. "Anyway, hedgehogs can't get through cat flaps. Their legs are too short."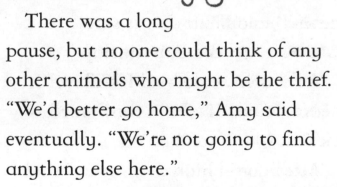

There was a long pause, but no one could think of any other animals who might be the thief. "We'd better go home," Amy said eventually. "We're not going to find anything else here."

"I'll walk with you," said Isambard.

When they got outside, they were surprised to find Willow and Einstein waiting for them. "Have you found the thief yet?" Willow asked eagerly.

"No," said Isambard, Plato and Hilton together.

"I'm sorry," said Amy. "We're no closer to solving the crime than we were before we started searching."

"Well, we all know what that means," said Willow.

"Do we?" asked Einstein.

"Of course we do," said Willow. "It means we were right in the first place. It's Bun who is stealing our food."

"I still don't think that's true," said Amy. "He says it wasn't him, and he's never told lies before."

"He's never stolen our food before either," said Isambard. "But he might be doing both now."

Einstein nodded in agreement. "The thief has got to be really greedy to eat three dinners in one night. And the only greedy animal I know is Bun."

Willow stood up straight and stuck her nose in the air. "I'm calling a meeting," she announced in a very important voice. "We can't help other people with a thief in our midst. It's time to throw Bun out of the Clamerkin Clan."

Amy stared at her in dismay. "We can't do that."

"Yes, we can," said Willow. "And if we don't, I'm going to leave."

"So am I," said Einstein.

"Me too," said Isambard.

Amy's eyes prickled with tears, and she blinked hard to stop herself crying. "Please don't leave," she begged. "And don't throw Bun out either. We need to stay together. The clan does such good things."

"But the clan can't help other people if we don't trust each other," said Hilton.

Plato hung his head sadly. "Maybe it's time to give it up completely."

All three cats refused to go and talk to Bun. So Amy, Hilton and Plato were left with the unpleasant task of telling him about the meeting and making sure that he went.

"Do we need an excuse to visit him?" said Hilton, when they reached the baker's shop.

"We did for the others," Plato agreed.

"This should do the job," said Amy, as she pulled out the piece of paper she'd put in her pocket earlier. She popped into the shop and handed it to the baker, who was as round as his cat and equally friendly. "Mum asked me to give you this order for tomorrow's bread."

Bun's human wiped the flour off his glasses and read the paper carefully. "The Primrose Tea Room must be doing well to need so many loaves."

"It is," said Amy. Then she asked, "Can I go and see Bun while I'm here?"

"Of course you can," said the baker with a smile. "It might cheer him up. He's been looking a bit down lately."

Amy, Hilton and Plato ran along the alleyway by the side of the shop and went in through the back door. Bun was delighted to see them, until they told him about the meeting. Amy was careful not to mention what it was about, but he guessed.

"They're going to be horrid to me. I know they are."

Amy bent down and stroked him as reassuringly as she could. She wanted to tell him that everything would be all right, but she couldn't. Without some evidence that Bun was innocent, the clan was going to break up.

She looked around the room and saw two bowls and a cat bed, just like she had everywhere else. Then she noticed something was missing. "Where's your cat flap?"

"I don't have one," said Bun. "I get in and out through there." He pointed at a window high up in the outside wall. "My human leaves it open all the time just for me."

Hilton looked at the window and then looked at Bun. Then he howled with laughter. "Surely you can't jump up there. Jumping's really energetic, and you're a bit…" He hesitated, obviously searching for the right word.

"Fat," suggested Plato helpfully. "Well built, plump, cuddly."

"Okay, I've got the message," said Bun. "And you're right about the jumping. That's why I climb."

Amy looked at the window again and noticed a pile of boxes below it arranged to make a neat set of steps. As she watched, Bun ran up them with surprising speed and balanced proudly on the edge of the opening.

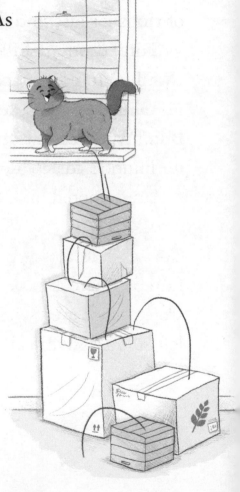

"My human leaves the boxes there all the time for me to use," the black cat explained. "Come and see what's outside. It's really clever." Then he disappeared through the window.

Amy, Hilton and Plato rushed out of the door just in time to see him walking down a narrow plank of wood that led from the window sill to the ground. It was a perfect cat ramp.

"That's neat," said Hilton.

"Flying's easier," said Plato.

Amy ignored him. She was too busy thinking. Had they finally found a clue? Could the fact that Bun didn't have a cat flap be the reason his food was never stolen — not even when he deliberately left some to tempt the thief?

CHAPTER 7

Bun was so unwilling to go to the
meeting that Amy had to carry him
there again. She put him down when
she sat on the grass in the almost-secret
hideout, but he wouldn't go near the
other cats. Instead he huddled as close
to her side as he could get. She could
feel his whole body shaking with
nerves.

Willow stood up and took control. "We're here to decide whether Bun can stay in the clan," she announced.

Bun whimpered and stared at Amy with huge, round eyes. "Don't let them throw me out," he pleaded.

"I'll do my best," Amy promised. Then she turned to the rest of the clan. "I think Bun's food isn't being stolen because he hasn't got a cat flap like the rest of you."

"I suppose that's possible," said Einstein.

"But it's only a guess," said Willow. "It doesn't prove that Bun is innocent."

Plato fluffed out his feathers importantly and said, "But it does provide reasonable doubt."

"What does that mean?" said Hilton. "Is it something else you've learned from the TV?"

"I don't care what it means," said Isambard with an angry twitch of his tail. "I'm not feeling reasonable.

I'm tired of having my food stolen."

"I think Plato's made a good point," said Amy. "There's always been some doubt about whether Bun is the thief and now there's even more. So I think we shouldn't rush into a decision. We should spend more time trying to find out the truth."

"By doing what?" asked Willow. "Nothing you've tried so far has helped."

Amy's shoulders slumped. All her ideas had failed, and she hadn't thought of any others. But she couldn't abandon Bun now and see the clan broken up for good. "Just give me more time," she begged. "I'm sure I'll think of something."

The three cats huddled together and had a brief whispered conversation. Then Willow stepped forward. "You can have until noon on Saturday," she announced. "But if you haven't found anything by then, either Bun leaves the clan or we do."

Amy gulped. It was already Thursday, and it was almost supper time. She only had two days to solve the crime, and she had no idea how she was going to do it.

Amy thought about the problem for
the rest of the day. She dreamed about
it all night, and she kept thinking
about it at school on Friday when she
should have been concentrating on her
lessons. But she still hadn't had any
ideas by the time school ended.

She set off for home feeling
absolutely miserable. She didn't want
the cats to have their dinners stolen
and go hungry. She didn't want Bun to
be unhappy, and she didn't want the
clan to break up. But she couldn't
think of any way to stop it all
happening.

The nearer she got to the Primrose
Tea Room, the slower she walked.
Hilton and Plato were going to be so

disappointed when they heard that she still didn't have a plan. The longer it took her to get home, the longer she could put off telling them.

Suddenly she heard a frantic yowling. It was a cat, and it was really unhappy. She raced along the road, trying to find the source of the sound. As she got closer, she could make out words, and she recognized the voice.

"Help, help!" screamed Isambard.

She hurtled around a corner and nearly crashed into Mr Jones. He was walking in the opposite direction, carrying a large plastic box with a metal grille on the front. It was a cat carrier, and the cat it was carrying was Isambard.

The tabby cat pressed his nose against the grille, pushed a paw through one of the holes and waved at Amy. "Save me!" he begged.

"What's wrong?" she asked.

Mr Jones assumed she was talking to him. "I think Isambard might be poorly. So I'm taking him to the vet."

"No, no," wailed Isambard. "Not the vet. I hate the vet. He prods me and pokes me and sticks needles in me."

"Calm down, old chap," said Mr Jones. He jiggled the cat carrier in what he obviously thought would be a reassuring manner. But it wasn't.

"Stop!" shrieked Isambard. "I want to go home."

Amy waited until he paused for

breath. Then she asked, "Why do you think your cat's ill?"

"He must be," said Mr Jones. "He's eating as much as usual, but he's losing weight."

"Tell him about the thief," Isambard pleaded. "Tell him my food's being stolen."

Amy hesitated. She wanted to help, but she couldn't tell Mr Jones that she knew what was happening. If she did, she'd have to explain how she knew and then her secret power wouldn't be secret any more.

"Please," begged the tabby cat. "Please, please, please."

Amy knew she must be very careful. So she smiled at Mr Jones and said,

"He might not be ill. There might be some other reason why Isambard's getting thinner."

"Like what?"

"Like another cat stealing his food when he's not looking."

Mr Jones frowned. "I suppose that's possible." Then he shook his head and said, "But I can't be sure. I'd better take him to the vet anyway, just to be on the safe side."

"No," wailed Isambard. "Amy! Save me!"

Amy desperately wanted to help, but she'd already done everything she could think of. If Plato was here, she was sure he'd suggest something he'd seen on TV. So she started thinking through everything she'd seen the police do in the crime shows.

They set traps. That hadn't helped.

They searched for clues. That hadn't helped either.

Then she remembered something else the police did – something she hadn't tried yet. And if it worked, it could prove Isambard's food was being stolen *and* find out who was stealing it.

CHAPTER 8

Amy smiled as reassuringly as she could at Isambard. Then she turned to Mr Jones and said, "The police on TV use security cameras to solve crimes. We can look at the pictures from the ones in your workshop to see what's happening to Isambard's food."

"That's an excellent idea, Amy," said Mr Jones. "There's just one problem."

Amy raised her eyebrows questioningly. "What's that?"

"I don't have any security cameras. There's never seemed much point when there's so little crime on Clamerkin Island."

"There's crime now," Isambard grumbled from inside the cat carrier. "Someone's stealing my dinner."

Mr Jones looked worried. "I can hear the poor cat's not happy. I'd better play it safe and take him to the vet."

"No!" wailed Isambard.

"You don't need to take him straight away," said Amy. "We could set up the camera on my tablet to watch his food tonight. Then you could take him to the vet tomorrow if it shows his food

isn't being stolen."
Mr Jones
peered
through the
grille at
Isambard,
who peered
back with
huge, pleading
eyes. "I suppose it
wouldn't do any harm to put off the vet
for just one day." Then he smiled at
Amy and said, "Come on then. Let's
try your idea."

Amy ran home to collect her tablet
and tell her parents where she was
going. Then she went back to the
workshop.

Isambard rubbed himself against her legs as she went inside. "Thanks, Amy. I hope this works."

"So do I," Amy whispered, so only the cat could hear.

She and Mr Jones spent the next hour making a stand to hold the tablet in the right position. Then they lined it up so the camera pointed at the food, plugged in the charger to make sure the battery didn't go flat and downloaded an app to make the tablet take a photograph every fifteen seconds right through the night. "That should definitely let us see the thief if there is one," said Mr Jones.

"I bet it's Bun," muttered Isambard.

Amy really hoped it wasn't.

The next morning was Saturday so there was no school. But Amy was up early anyway. She was keen to solve the mystery of the disappearing dinners, and Mr Jones had promised not to look at the pictures until she got there.

As Amy ran down the road with Hilton and Plato, the parrot was even more excited than she was. "We're being real detectives," he said.

Mr Jones was waiting for them. "I think it worked all right," he said as he switched on the tablet. Then he propped it up on his desk so it was easy to see.

A clear picture of Isambard's food

bowl appeared on the screen. Then another one and another and another. The pictures kept changing, but they were all exactly the same.

Hilton yawned. "This is boring," he grumbled.

"It's like the worst TV programme ever," squawked Plato. "Perhaps the thief didn't come."

"He must have done," said Isambard. "My food had all gone this morning, and it wasn't me who ate it."

Suddenly Amy shouted, "Stop!"

Mr Jones froze the picture and they all looked at it carefully. In the bottom right-hand corner of the screen was something white and furry.

"It looks like a paw," said Amy.

"It's not Isambard's," said Mr Jones.
"Maybe you're right about there being
a thief."

"Look at the next picture," squawked
Plato, bouncing from foot to foot in
excitement.

"Is your parrot all right?" said Mr Jones, who couldn't understand what Plato was saying.

"He's fine," said Amy. "Let's look at the next picture."

Mr Jones tapped the screen and the thief finally came into view. Standing in front of Isambard's bowl was a roly-poly puppy covered in white fur.

"Martha!" said Hilton and Amy together.

"Who?" said Mr Jones, Isambard and Plato.

"She's Mrs Taylor's new puppy,"
Amy explained. "But I'm sure she's not
allowed to wander. How can she be
getting out?"

Mr Jones picked up the tablet and
headed for the door. "Come on," he
said. "We'd better find out."

Mrs Taylor was shocked when they
showed her the pictures. "She must
have escaped through the cat flap in
the kitchen. It was
already here when
I moved in, and I
didn't realize
she could get
through." Then
she wagged a finger

disapprovingly at Martha and said, "You are a very bad puppy."

Martha licked the finger and bounced happily onto Mrs Taylor's lap. "Iggle, oggle, din-dins," she said.

"I think she's too young to understand that she's done anything wrong," said Amy. "All you can do is make sure she stays at home in future."

"I'll come around later with some tools," said Mr Jones. "I'm sure I can fasten that flap so she can't get out."

Amy left the adults talking and went outside with Hilton and Plato. Then they split up. Hilton ran to tell Isambard, Willow and Einstein who the thief really was, while Amy and

Plato went to give the good news to Bun.

The black cat was thrilled. Amy had never seen him so happy. "It's wonderful," he mewed, as he bounded around Amy like a kitten. Then he rolled on his back and waved his paws in the air with pleasure.

This time he didn't need any encouragement to go to the meeting. He trotted beside Amy, purring loudly. But when they reached the bushes at the end of her garden, he hesitated and looked anxiously at Amy. "Are you sure everything's going to be all right?"

"Absolutely sure," said Amy, with her fingers crossed behind her back in the hope that it would be.

Neither of them needed to have worried. As Bun stepped into the almost-secret meeting place, the other three cats rushed to greet him. Then they stopped and hung their heads in shame.

"We're sorry," said Einstein. "We should have believed you."

"We've been mean and horrid," said Isambard.

"Especially me," said Willow. "Please forgive us."

"Of course I will," said Bun. "Let's forget all about it and be friends again."

Amy watched happily as the four cats snuggled up to each other. It was good to know that the quarrel was over, and the clan was safe.

Bun gave a contented sigh. "This is perfect," he purred. "The only thing that could make it even better would be a sardine."

Amy laughed. "I think I can manage that," she said.

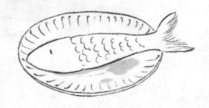

For more animal hide-and-seek games, try Usborne Look and Find Cats & Dogs

Illustration by Gareth Lucas

LOOK OUT FOR MORE AMY WILD ADVENTURES...

AMY WILD

AND THE SILLY SQUIRREL

When Casper the squirrel tells the Clamerkin Clan that his oak-tree home is going to be cut down, Amy and her friends jump into action. Can they come up with a plan to save the tree and all the birds and animals who live there?